Stalker

by

Anthony Masters

First published in Great Britain by Barrington Stoke Ltd
10 Belford Terrace, Edinburgh EH4 3DQ
Copyright © 2002 Anthony Masters

This edition is based on *Stalker*, published by Barrington Stoke in 1999

The moral right of the author has been asserted in
accordance with the Copyright, Designs and
Patents Act 1988

ISBN 1-84299-081-0

Printed by Polestar AUP Aberdeen Ltd

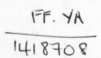

A Note from the Author

We're all afraid of being followed. I remember walking home from the station when I was in my teens. The night was dark and foggy. I could hear some footsteps behind me – they were soft and shuffling at first but after a while they began to ring out on the pavement.

I couldn't see anyone in the swirling fog. I checked my watch – 10 p.m. The street was empty. My heart was thumping. I was sweating.

I began to walk faster. The footsteps behind me became faster. I looked round again, but there was still no-one there.

Then I saw the bus shelter. To my joy I saw people standing there, waiting for the bus. I crossed the road to join them. I looked back – still no-one came.

Maybe the person had taken the path over the common.

Or maybe they weren't following me after all?

To Robina – as always, the light
of my life – with much love

Contents

1	Trapped	1
2	Rescue	9
3	Threat	13
4	Escape	19
5	Spying	23
6	Crash	29
7	Drop	37
8	Knife	43
9	Anne	49
10	Footsteps	57
11	Testing	63

Chapter 1
Trapped

"I'm leaving," said Sarah.

"You're what?" Chris was horrified.

He gripped the spanner tightly. His knuckles showed white. For a moment Sarah wondered if he was going to hit her.

"I'm leaving," she repeated. "I want out."

"From the job?"

"From everything," she replied firmly.

"Including me?" asked Chris. "You can't do that."

"Just watch me then. I want out. I'm fed up with your temper and I'm fed up with the job."

"In that order?" asked Chris.

"In that order."

"There's someone else, isn't there?"

Sarah looked at her watch. It was well after half-past six and everybody else had gone home, leaving Chris to lock up.

Sarah's job was to book in the cars and do most of the office paperwork. She sometimes stayed late to catch up. That's how she got to know Chris, the mechanic, alone together in the empty building. He always stayed late to lock up.

"Yes, there's someone else," said Sarah.

She hadn't planned to break it to him like this, but their relationship had got so bad she didn't care what she said.

Sarah had only met Tim a few weeks ago, but, for the first time, she knew what it was like to be really happy. Tim respected her, made Sarah feel a real person.

Chris was jealous if Sarah as much as looked at another man. Worse still, he had threatened to hit her several times. Sarah had decided she was not going to put up with him any longer. She needed to make a clean break.

Chris was standing close to her now, the spanner raised. "Who is he?" Chris demanded.

"I'm not telling you," Sarah replied.

"I'll kill him," shouted Chris.

Chris was short and stocky and with his crew-cut and bulging arm muscles, he looked aggressive.

"Don't be stupid," Sarah yelled back.

"You belong to me."

"I don't *belong* to anyone," Sarah said sharply.

"I love you."

"You don't love me. You've never loved me. You just want to own me like you own a car."

"We can start again." Chris's voice shook.

"It's too late now. I've got to go."

"You're not going anywhere."

Sarah could see the sweat standing out on his forehead and the little pulse beating in his cheek. Suddenly, she felt frightened.

"I'm going home now," she said.

"I told you – you're not going anywhere."

Chris stood in front of her, blocking her way. Chris was a good mechanic, but he'd never had any confidence. He still lived with his mum. He was her only son, and she loved him so much that she spoilt him. His dad had walked out years ago and Chris was all she had.

Now he grabbed Sarah by the arm and pulled her towards the office.

"Let me go!" Sarah shouted. "You need time to cool off."

Chris was half dragging her now, hurting her arm. If only the boss hadn't gone home early. If only one last customer would come. But it was now well after closing time and Sarah felt really scared.

"Get in that office." Chris dragged open the door.

"No way." Sarah was resisting him.

He pushed her hard and Sarah fell backwards onto the office carpet. Chris stood over her. The spanner was still in his hand.

"I'm going to lock you in until I've finished my last job. Think hard. Then we'll talk again. You'll change your mind."

"No, I won't." Sarah was determined not to cry or show how afraid she was. "I want out."

Chris's lips moved, but no sound came. Sarah knew his rage was getting worse. "Think it over." He grabbed the office key, slammed the door and locked her in.

Sarah knew she was trapped and at Chris's mercy. What was she going to do? Then she realised that he had forgotten about the phone. She picked it up and dialled a number she knew by heart.

****

"Tim?" she said softly.

"Speak up. I can't hear you." He was home.

"I can't. It's Sarah."

"What are you whispering for?" Tim's voice was steady and calm.

"Chris has locked me in the office at the garage." Sarah was speaking as loudly as she dared.

"What for?"

"I told him about us."

"You managed to come clean with him at last."

There was joy in Tim's voice but concern too. "How did he take it?"

"Badly." Sarah sounded really upset.

"He hasn't hurt you?" Tim said, worried.

"Not yet."

"What's that supposed to mean?"
Tim sounded uneasy.

"He's locked me in the office and I'm
scared, Tim. Really scared."

"I'm coming straight over, Sarah." Tim was
as forceful as ever.

"Be quick. Please, please be quick."

"I'll be with you in five minutes. I'll come
on my bike."

"Be careful of Chris," she warned.

Tim worked as an electrician in town.
They had met at a club and had clicked at
once. He was good-looking and he had a great
sense of humour. He didn't look as if he
would *ever* take Sarah for granted. Not like
Chris. And he was coming over right now.

Chapter 2
Rescue

Tim roared up on his motorbike. He parked in front of the workshop entrance and went straight in.

"Anybody about?" he said, looking around.

"We're closed," said Chris, crawling out from underneath a car.

"I've come to see Sarah Jackson."

"Who are you, then?" asked Chris.

"Tim. I'm Sarah's boyfriend and I've come to collect her."

There was a long silence which seemed to go on for ever.

Then Chris said, "You've got that wrong. You're not her boyfriend. I am."

"You're a bit out of touch, aren't you? Things have changed." Tim was smiling.

"Get out," yelled Chris.

"I'm not going anywhere." Tim raised his voice. "Sarah – you around?"

"I'm in the office," she called back. "Chris locked me in."

"That wasn't a very nice thing to do, was it?" said Tim. He was taller than Chris, but not as heavily built. "Now will you please give me the key so I can take Sarah home?"

"Come and get it," said Chris, taking a swing at Tim who dodged.

10

Chris tried again, but Tim grabbed his arm and threw him backwards. Chris fell over a bench and a load of tools clattered down on him. He rolled over and tried to get to his feet, but Tim kicked out, catching him in the stomach. He doubled up, winded, gasping for air.

"Did you say you had that key?" asked Tim.

Chris continued to gasp for breath.

Tim stood over him.

"Wait!" groaned Chris.

"I'm in a hurry," warned Tim.

"Here's the key." Chris took it from his pocket and threw it on the floor.

Tim picked it up and hurried over to the office. He unlocked the door and Sarah came out. She gazed down at Chris who had risen to his knees, still clutching at his stomach.

"I think we should make a quick getaway," said Tim.

****

Sarah and Tim ducked under the steel shutter at the workshop entrance. He unhooked his tank-bag and pulled out a crash helmet for her.

"Let's go!" yelled Tim, starting the engine. "Like fast."

Sarah clambered onto the back of the bike. She gripped Tim round the waist.

Just then Chris made a rush at them, the spanner gripped tightly in his hand. "I'll get you for this. I'll get you both," he shouted, as Tim rode the bike away with Sarah's head pressed into his shoulder.

The spanner went flying over her head.

"Right nutter," yelled Tim.

Chapter 3
Threat

When they got back to Tim's flat, Sarah was in a state of shock. "What did you *do* to him?" she asked.

"Roughed him up a little," said Tim, not in the least worried.

"You've no idea how jealous Chris can be." Sarah was terrified. "He'll come round to my house."

"Will he hurt you?" Tim was alarmed now.

"I just don't know."

"How about going away for a few days?" Tim suggested.

"Where?"

"Cornwall?"

"I can't afford to pay for a hotel," Sarah objected.

"You won't have to. Don't you remember me saying I was brought up there? Dad and Mum still have a holiday cottage down there. There's no-one in it right now. We could start off tomorrow."

"What about your job?" asked Sarah.

"I can take a few days off. They can cope without me."

"At such short notice?"

"I can fix it." Tim put his arms round Sarah and kissed her. "Why don't you stop worrying and leave this to me?"

Sarah nodded. "But what about tonight? My parents are going out. Suppose Chris comes round? What am I going to do?"

"Stay here with me."

"But Mum might not like the idea – "

For the first time Tim got cross. She saw a cold look in his eyes which she'd never seen before. Sarah was surprised. Then the look disappeared.

"Do you want me to talk to your parents? Surely they know about Chris's temper?"

Sarah lived with her parents. She was an only child and they fussed over her. Her dad insisted that she told him everything.

"They've always been worried about Chris," she said.

Sarah was beginning to get uneasy. Tim was going too fast. He was making all the decisions for both of them and she felt helpless. But he *had* rescued her.

He went to the phone and began to dial.

"You remembered my number," she said, pleased.

"I want to help you," said Tim briskly. "We need to sort this out. Like now." He was sounding like her dad.

Sarah listened in amazement as Tim talked to her father. He sounded so convincing. He got straight to the point and spoke to her father frankly.

"The problem is that Chris has been threatening Sarah," Tim told him. "And I'm really worried."

Tim paused and listened to Sarah's dad. "You say he's threatened Sarah before? You've never thought that he would do anything?"

Tim paused again. "Oh, I see – you do now. Well, you'll be pleased to hear Sarah's leaving the job at the garage, so what if I took her away for a few days? My parents have got a holiday cottage in Cornwall and we could both go down there and have a break. I mean – I realise you haven't known me long, but ..."

He held the phone closer to his ear. "Sorry? You think it's a good idea too? That's great. Suppose she stays here tonight and we go down early tomorrow morning?"

Sarah watched Tim as he nodded confidently. "You know I'll look after her, Mr Jackson," he told her father. "And I'm sorry we've only met briefly. But now that things have changed, maybe I could come and have a longer chat with you when we're back from Cornwall. Good. I'll look forward to it."

He put down the phone with a wink and a thumbs up to Sarah.

Sarah realised that Tim had fixed everything. She felt thankful. At least one problem was solved.

Chapter 4

Escape

Sarah lay in Tim's arms that night. She was thinking. How had Tim managed to convince her father that she should both stay the night and go down to Cornwall with him? Her parents, particularly her dad, worried about her all the time. Did he really think Tim was safe? Or was it just that he was so much safer than Chris?

"Do you think – " Sarah began.

"If you're going to start talking about Chris again – don't bother. He'll cool off when he's got used to the idea you've *really* left him." Tim drew Sarah to him and kissed her on the lips. "Stop worrying," he said. "We're going to have a ball."

Next morning, Sarah and Tim rode his bike down to the cottage in Cornwall. They called in at Sarah's house first. There was no-one in. She hurriedly packed some things in a rucksack. Soon they were on their way, the threat of violence from Chris forgotten.

Sarah held on tight to Tim, feeling the wind in her face. He rode fast but carefully. They stopped twice to stretch their legs. Over a quick lunch in a café, they smiled happily. They were really getting to know each other.

****

Tim and Sarah arrived at Langton Cove at about six. They did not go straight to the cottage. Tim parked the bike in the small car park at the top of the hill and padlocked it. Then he and Sarah walked hand-in-hand down to the harbour. The early summer evening was warm and they sat down on the wall to watch the most wonderful sunset.

Sarah nodded off, her head on Tim's shoulder.

He kissed her and said, "Let's go to the cottage and raid the fridge. Then we can have an early night."

****

They returned to the bike and rode slowly along the steep, cobbled street and turned into a side road. His parents' cottage was small and thatched. The door had a brass knocker in the shape of a Cornish pixie.

Once inside, Sarah found the rooms cosy and comfortable. She lay on the bed, listening to the sound of the sea, more relaxed than she had been for months. Downstairs she could hear Tim preparing supper.

Chris didn't know how to boil an egg and she always had to wait on him. Now, at last, Sarah had met someone who was going to wait on her.

After a tasty fry-up of sausage, bacon and egg, they went to bed together. She had never felt so safe or so happy as she slipped between the sheets beside Tim.

Chapter 5

Spying

Next morning, Sarah got up, opened the curtains and gazed out at the cobbled street that led down to the sparkling sea.

"It's a lovely day," she said. "Why don't we have an early morning swim?"

But Tim only grunted and turned over in bed.

"Lazybones!" She laughed and ran over and kissed him on his unshaven chin.

Sarah hurried down the stairs and went into the kitchen, filled the kettle and put it on to boil. Then she pulled open the front door, stood on the step and breathed in the sea air.

After a while, she went back inside. Sarah noticed a folded slip of paper lying on the floor. Someone must have pushed it through the letterbox, she thought, as she smoothed out the note.

Then she gasped in horror and shock.

The note read: *YOU'RE DEAD.*

Sarah screamed and in seconds a rumpled Tim was standing by her side. "What is it?"

"Look at this." She passed him the note with a shaking hand. "Chris must have written that."

Tim read the note silently.

"He can't have followed us all the way down here. Besides, he wouldn't know the address," he said.

"He could have found out."

"Don't be stupid, Sarah." Tim's voice was sharp. "After all your dad said about Chris, he's not likely to have told him our address, is he? And he doesn't know where my parents live to ask them."

Sarah had to agree. Then she said, "Suppose he followed us in his car?"

"We'd have seen him."

"He could have been careful."

"Sure." Tim was still staring down at the note. Then he shoved it in his pocket. Suddenly his expression changed. "Wait a minute." He went to the front door and flung it open.

"What is it?" Sarah asked, alarmed.

Tim didn't reply as he hurried outside.

Dark thoughts raced through Sarah's mind. Someone was watching them, spying on them, following them everywhere. She had read about stalkers in the newspapers. Could this be happening to them?

Tim had chained his motorbike to a lamp post when they had arrived. It was still there, but the bike had been attacked with some heavy object. There were dents in the petrol tank. The speedo was smashed and a headlight was broken.

Tim swore and Sarah stared at the damage, shivering. Maybe the stalker was a vandal too?

"Chris – " she muttered. "But how – "

Then Tim said, "Of course, it doesn't have to be Chris."

"What do you mean?"

Tim looked at Sarah thoughtfully, as if he was wondering if he could tell her something. Then he said, "I had a spot of bother down here last Christmas."

"What kind of bother?"

"About a girl." He was mumbling now, speaking fast, wanting to get it over.
"This – this local guy – Jake. He was an old childhood friend. Now he hates me. I thought he'd moved away, but maybe he's still around."

"He'd do something like this?" She was staring down at the damage.

"He might."

"And the note?" Sarah sounded upset.

"Just to frighten us."

Could there be someone else around with a temper like Chris? It didn't seem possible.

Tim was silent at breakfast and Sarah felt there was a barrier between them.

Several times she tried to break it down and failed. Then she asked, "You going to the police?"

"What's the point?" he snapped.

"They'll arrest this Jake person."

"They won't have any proof," he pointed out.

"You could explain everything," she suggested.

"No chance."

"But how are you going to pay for the damage?" she asked.

"I'll manage. Now leave me alone."

Tim seemed angry with her.

Chapter 6
Crash

As they strolled around Langton Cove, Tim barely spoke, his face white and strained, cold and remote. Sarah felt cut out.

They ended up later that morning, sitting again on the harbour wall. They stared out at the calm sea. The sky was cloudy. The waves made little slapping noises on the stony beach and a radio blared pop music from one of the fishing boats.

Sarah felt as grey and depressed as the sea and sky. Somehow her mood even spoilt the view.

Then Tim said, "I'm sorry." He took Sarah's hand. "I paid a lot of money for that bike."

"I know. But are you *sure* it couldn't have been Chris?"

"The odds are against him – particularly if Jake's around."

"Where does he live?" Sarah asked.

"On a farm out in the country. A couple of miles from here," Tim told her.

"Why don't we go and see him?"

"No chance." Tim sounded gloomy.

"But why not?"

"There'd be trouble."

They sat in silence.

****

"I thought I might find you here," said a voice with a Cornish accent. Sarah quickly turned round and saw a slight, thin boy with a mass of red hair.

Tim looked completely taken aback. Then he switched on a sarcastic smile. "This is Jake," Tim said shakily. "Meet Sarah."

Tim and Jake looked at each other uneasily.

"I thought you'd gone to that job in Devon," snapped Tim.

"It didn't work out," said Jake.

"So?" Tim didn't sound too sure of himself.

"I came back to work on the farm."

There was a long pause during which Sarah looked from Tim to Jake. Neither of them gave much away, but she could sense their dislike for each other. Sarah felt afraid.

She was not sure what to do. Tim seemed different, as if he was a stranger again.

"What do you want?" asked Tim uneasily. Sarah wondered why he didn't mention the smashed-up bike.

"It doesn't get any easier," said Jake.

"What doesn't?" asked Sarah boldly.

"Did you know he killed my sister?" Jake spoke so quietly she could hardly hear him.

Everything seemed to stop. Even the clouds in the sky no longer blew across the sun. Sarah couldn't hear anything but Jake's question. *Did you know he killed my sister?*

Then life returned to normal. The waves slapped at the pebbles, the noisy radio from the fishing boat blared and seagulls shrieked as they flew overhead.

Sarah looked at Tim but he was silent.

Eventually he mumbled, "You know what happened was an accident."

"I don't see it like that." Jake's voice was flat.

"Did you wreck Tim's motorbike?" asked Sarah, determined to challenge him.

Jake looked at her, puzzled. "Of course I didn't."

"Did you put a note through the door of his parents' cottage?"

"No."

"A note that said, *YOU'RE DEAD*," she went on.

"I'm not that childish."

"And yet you're accusing Tim of killing your sister."

Sarah was wondering why Tim wasn't angry. If he could stand up to Chris, why couldn't he stand up to Jake, who looked such a wimp?

"That's right." Jake's face was full of hatred and Sarah felt a stab of fear. "He killed my sister, Anne."

"OK. Let's get this sorted out." Tim seemed to be back in control and Sarah felt more confident. "Maybe I should have told you this but I suppose the memory was too raw. I used to go out with Jake's sister, Anne. One night she and I were coming back from a club and the car skidded off the road in a rain storm. The police cleared me. Anne's parents cleared me. They all knew it was an accident. The only person who wouldn't clear me was Jake. Anyway, that's why I bought the bike. I couldn't drive a car again – not ever – not after what happened."

Tim sounded close to tears, but Jake just stared at him with scorn.

"You killed her, Tim. You'll always have to live with that – and you know it." Jake turned away and then glanced back at Sarah. "Be careful. Tim's dangerous. Most of all with women."

As Jake hurried away, Tim said to Sarah, "I reckon Anne's death drove him mad."

"What did her death do to you?"

"Bad things."

"Why didn't you tell me before?" asked Sarah.

"I couldn't. I'm trying to put Anne behind me. Do you understand?"

"Were you hurt in the crash?"

"Only bumped and bruised. Anne wasn't wearing a seat-belt and she went through the window." Tim's eyes filled with tears and his voice broke. "You've got to help me, Sarah."

"I will," she said, putting her arms round him. "You've helped me so much. I want to do the same for you."

Tim gave a dry sob. "One day I'll be able to talk about what happened."

"I'll be here," Sarah said, comforting him.

Chapter 7
Drop

That afternoon, Tim and Sarah went for a long walk over the cliffs. The path climbed steeply and they could hear the sea far below.

"Was Jake close to his sister?" she asked.

Tim seemed to be calmer and more confident now. "Very."

"What about Anne?"

"She adored him. I always thought they were too close."

"Do you think Jake smashed up your bike?"

"It's possible."

"And the note?"

Tim shrugged and was silent. Sarah was determined to keep going.

"*Could* it be Jake who's been stalking us?" Sarah asked.

"He's been very unhappy for a long time. If I'd known he was back down here I'd never have suggested coming."

"We're torn between the devil and the deep blue sea," said Sarah.

"What's that meant to mean?"

"It's an old saying. We're torn between Chris with all his threats, and Jake with all his hatred."

They were standing on the highest part of the cliff, watching the waves hit the reef that ran out to sea far below. There was a hollow booming sound and great sheets of spray rose up towards them.

"Don't let's go too near," said Sarah.

But Tim was already on the edge, a smile on his lips. "It's wonderful, isn't it?"

"I'm frightened of steep drops like this," whispered Sarah. "They make me feel giddy."

"Come a bit closer and you'll get the thrill of your life."

That was the last thing Sarah wanted, but she edged forward a little and Tim put his arms round her. "Now what do you think?" asked Tim.

Sarah gazed down at the lashing water and the jagged rocks. Her heart was pounding. "Let me go, Tim," she pleaded. "I hate being so close to the edge."

Tim laughed. "If it wasn't for me, you could fall."

"Let go," Sarah begged.

Tim pulled her back and kissed Sarah on the cheek. "I'm sorry. I didn't mean to frighten you."

She shivered. "It's just so far down. It really scares me."

"I like it. I feel I'm in control. One slip and – "

"That's just what scares me," she said as they walked slowly back towards the path.

****

"I'll go out and get us a bottle of wine," said Tim after Sarah had said it was her turn to make supper for them both tonight. Tim had agreed reluctantly. She wondered if he thought she couldn't even cook a proper meal.

Sarah felt nervous. There could be no doubt that Tim liked to be in control of everything. Sarah uneasily remembered the cliff-top and the terrible drop. She shivered. Maybe he was *too* protective. But wasn't that what she really wanted from a man? Protection?

Sarah felt ashamed as she began to roll out pastry for a pie. Why was she so weak?

As she began to chop up some mushrooms, Sarah cut her finger. She hurried up to the bedroom, wondering where she would find a plaster. She felt stupid. Tim would never have cut himself. He was too organised for that.

Sarah thought she had seen a packet of plasters in a top drawer and she sorted through it, trying to keep her bleeding finger away from Tim's sweaters. Then she felt something hard and sharp. Slowly Sarah pulled out a knife.

Chapter 8
Knife

Why should Tim have hidden a knife in the drawer? It didn't seem a bit like him. Or was it? Tim made plans. Tim was so organised and – whether she liked it or not – he was very protective. The devil and the deep blue sea. He was between the two. Chris and Jake. Jake and Chris. Both angry. Both after her.

So Tim *did* think one of them was capable of attacking his bike. Then there was the note. *YOU'RE DEAD.* The terrible words repeated themselves over and over again in Sarah's mind. *YOU'RE DEAD – YOU'RE –*

The doorbell rang and she peered down from the upstairs window. Jake was standing on the doorstep.

****

The bell rang again as Sarah ran down the stairs. She shouldn't let him in. It was clear Tim had hidden the knife to protect them both from Jake. So what was she doing, going to open the front door to the enemy?

But Sarah wanted to find out more about Jake. She needed to take a risk. "What is it?" she demanded as she opened the front door.

"I want to talk," said Jake.

"But Tim will be back any minute," she objected.

"He's in the pub. I haven't got much time."

"Has he seen you?" asked Sarah.

"No. Look – you've got to trust me. I want to talk to you. I'm not going to hurt you."

I'd be a fool to let Jake in, Sarah thought. Tim would be deeply angry.

But she *had* to know more. "You haven't got long," she said.

At first Sarah wished she'd brought the knife with her as she led Jake into the kitchen. But then she wouldn't have known how to use it.

She heard Jake speaking to her urgently. "Tim killed my sister."

"It was an accident," she replied.

"It only *looked* like an accident. He killed her before the crash and then he burnt the car."

Sarah gazed at Jake. He looked normal. But what he was saying was crazy.

"Tim didn't tell me there was a fire." Sarah was puzzled.

"Tim hasn't told you much."

"He wants to look after me," she said firmly.

"He wants to keep you under his control."

"I don't understand." Sarah remembered what had happened on the cliff-top when Tim had pulled her so near to the edge.

"He wants to possess you like he possessed Anne," Jake insisted.

"He loves me," she replied.

"He's not capable of loving. Only possessing."

"How do you know all this?" asked Sarah.

"Anne told me."

"This is crazy," mocked Sarah. "It's you who's sick. Leaving that note. Attacking his bike."

"If you ask me – " began Jake.

"I didn't."

"I reckon he attacked his *own* bike and wrote the note himself – so it would look as if I did it."

"He'd smash up his own bike?"

"I wouldn't put that past him. If only I'd listened to Anne. She was terrified of him. But I thought what she said was over the top. Anyway I'd got problems of my own at the time. So I didn't really listen to her. I was a fool. You've got to go back to London. I'll help you. I've got the car – "

There was a rattling of a key in the front door and Tim stepped into the hall. He was back from the pub. His voice was slurred as he called out, "Sarah – I'm home."

Chapter 9
Anne

Jake ran for the back door, but he was too late. Tim strode across the kitchen and grabbed him by the neck. Then he bent Jake's arm up behind his back and pushed him against the dresser. Sarah's pie went flying onto the floor.

"Why did you let him in?" Tim snarled. She had never seen him in such a rage before.

"I didn't know what to do," said Sarah miserably.

Jake gave a howl of pain as Tim increased the pressure on his arm.

"What's he been saying?" Tim looked at Sarah accusingly.

"Nothing. He's only just arrived."

"What do you want?" yelled Tim.

"To say I was sorry," gasped Jake. He was clearly terrified. "I got screwed up about Anne's death. Now – let – go – of – my – arm," he shouted in pain.

Tim seemed to check himself and suddenly released Jake. "Now get out," he ordered.

"OK. I'm going." Jake was backing off.

"If I see you here again, I'll really do something I'll regret."

"Will you?" Jake sounded more confident.

"I'll smack you one," Tim warned.

"Is that all?" Jake seemed more aggressive now. But he quickly left, slamming the door.

An odd and unsettling thought crossed Sarah's mind. Tim's manner reminded her of someone. Then she remembered. He reminded her of Chris.

When Jake had gone, Tim came back into the kitchen and asked, "Is that *all* he said?"

"Yes."

"You should *never* have let him in."

Tim was still angry, but Sarah felt less afraid of him now. Even so, she knew she needed to be careful.

"I know, I'm sorry. I got a bit upset."

"You're a silly old thing, aren't you?"

He took Sarah into his arms and began to kiss her. Tim had never called her a silly old thing before. Sarah found it rather insulting.

"Supper's going to be late," she said, pulling away from him and staring down at the mess on the floor.

"Let's have some fish and chips instead. We'll go and get them together." Tim paused. "I'm not leaving you on your own again. Not with Jake around."

Sarah drew back further. He didn't seem protective any longer. Instead he sounded as if he owned her – just like Chris.

****

"I love you," said Tim as they lay in bed that night. "I love you so much. I'll never love anyone else."

"This Anne – " asked Sarah. She was trying to get a bit more out of Tim. "How much did you love her?"

"I was very fond of her, but she wouldn't really – " Tim suddenly fell silent.

"She wouldn't what?"

"She wouldn't love me back. You're the only one who's done that."

Suddenly Tim looked almost helpless in the moonlit bedroom. This was a side of him that Sarah hadn't seen before. He was like a little lost boy and all her fears suddenly disappeared. "I love you, Tim. I'll never leave you."

"Promise?"

"Of course. We've been through so much together already and yet – "

"Yet what?" He sounded as if he didn't trust her.

"We hardly know each other."

"Give it time," he assured her. "Give *me* time."

Sarah lay awake for some time puzzling over the events of the day. But at last she fell into an uneasy sleep.

****

Sarah woke suddenly to the smell of burning. When she turned to where Tim had been lying beside her, the sheets were cold. He had gone.

She got up and ran to the top of the stairs. Clouds of smoke were drifting up from below. There was a deepening smell of burning. A little flame was crackling along the edge of the carpet in the hall. She could also see what she thought was broken glass on the floor.

Sarah ran back to the bedroom. She dragged a thick blanket off the bed and hurried down the stairs to smother the fire.

She stood watching the smoke die back. It made her choke.

"Tim?" she shouted. "Tim! Where are you?"

Sarah shouted again, but there was still no reply. Then she saw the front door was slightly open, and broken glass was scattered across the floor.

She checked the letterbox which was wide enough to push a bottle through. Suppose someone had filled the bottle with petrol and struck a match? She wondered if Tim had woken up and gone outside to chase the fire-raiser? Was it the stalker again? But why hadn't Tim put the flames out before he left? She could have been burnt to death. Had he not cared about her at all?

Then Sarah forgot that Tim was acting oddly and began to worry about him. Why didn't he come back? Had he been attacked? Knocked out? Was Tim lying in some back street of Langton Cove bleeding to death?

She decided to go out and search for him. After all, the village was small enough, wasn't it? Surely she wouldn't take long to find him.

Glancing down at her watch, Sarah saw it was 2 a.m. She checked the fire was finally out, she made sure she had a key and locked the front door carefully behind her. She ran down the lane. Then she paused. She did not know if she should go down the hill towards the sea or up the cobbled street to the top of the village.

Sarah thought she could hear footsteps. Could this be the stalker following her? She turned round to find there was no-one there. But when she started off again she was sure she could see a shadow moving between the cottages.

There was a yowl and a cat ran across the road. Sarah shivered nervously. She strode on, trying to tell herself it might just be all in her mind. Then she heard the footsteps again. There could be no doubt this time.

Chapter 10
Footsteps

Now Sarah was *sure* she was being followed. She began to run. So did the footsteps. When Sarah slowed down, the footsteps slowed down too. What *was* she going to do?

She was stiff with fear, her heart pumping.

Who *was* her stalker? Any moment now she could be raped or murdered. Maybe she only had a few minutes to live and they would find her body in the gutter, soaked in blood.

Forcing herself to stand still, Sarah turned round.

She let out a scream when she saw the familiar figure in a leather jacket. Chris's face was dead white in the moonlight.

****

"What are *you* doing here?" Sarah asked fearfully.

"I've got to talk to you," Chris begged.

"What about?" There was something different about him, she thought. He seemed more together than she had ever seen him.

"About Tim."

"Did you follow us down here?" Sarah asked angrily.

"I had a problem getting the address of the cottage. But in the end I traced that telephone call you made from the garage. Then I checked with a few of Tim's friends. I soon found out where you were."

"Did you smash up his bike and push that note under the door and set fire – " she began asking him.

"I don't know what you're talking about. I've only just got here. But I was in the pub earlier – the one by the harbour."

Sarah could see that Chris was telling the truth. But she was angry with him.

"So?" she demanded.

"I was asking about Tim, trying to find out who knew him. This guy Jake did."

"I suppose he told you about his sister," Sarah said.

"Yes. He also told me Tim had a real problem coping with relationships. That he used to test Anne out in all kinds of ways – to see how she'd react."

"What kinds of ways?" Sarah asked urgently.

"Anne kept getting these notes. They were never signed but she guessed who they were from. Once Tim took her so near the cliff edge that she was scared stiff."

Sarah felt a sick, cold feeling inside.

"He wants to own women, to control them. But he can never really trust anyone so he has to keep testing – to see how far he can go. The guy's sick, Sarah. Really sick."

She stared at Chris, not wanting to believe him.

Then Chris said, in a pleading tone. "OK. I know I was jealous too – and possessive – and I've got a temper. I'm sorry. It was my fault. But you *must* listen to me."

"You locked me in the office," said Sarah. "You threatened Tim and me."

"Look – I'm the jealous type, and I'll work on it, right? But Tim goes beyond all that. Don't you see? Jake said he tried to warn you,

but you wouldn't listen. I'm begging you,
Sarah. You've *got* to listen. Tim needs help."

Chapter 11
Testing

Sarah sat at the kitchen table, waiting for Tim to come home. She looked around her. She already loved the cottage. But she also realised she had only been pretending to feel at home here. In fact they had both been playing at keeping house together. But the game had become deadly.

The front door opened and Sarah jumped. She forced herself to stay sitting at the table. "Where have you been?" she asked.

"Looking for the fire-raiser," snapped Tim.

"Pity you didn't wake me and put the fire out before you left. I could have been burnt to death while I was asleep."

"But I did put it out." Tim paused and looked away, not wanting to make eye contact. "I'm sorry. It must have got going again."

Sarah said nothing, not knowing how to begin. Then she forced herself to continue. She hoped Tim could explain everything.

"What are you trying to do to me, Tim?" She wanted him to convince her – just as he had convinced her father.

"Sorry?" Tim looked at her blankly and Sarah prayed that Jake and Chris had been wrong.

"Why all this testing?"

"I don't understand."

"The note, and the fire. Why did you smash up your own bike? Did you want to prove to me I was surrounded by enemies? Did you want me to believe Chris and Jake were going to harm me? Did you want me to think that *you* were the only person who could love and protect me?"

"Are you crazy?" Tim whispered.

"No. You're the crazy one," she almost shouted. "Why couldn't you let everything happen naturally? Why do you need to build yourself up like this, playing tricks and games? I would have loved you. I didn't need all that. I wouldn't have gone back to Chris."

"Who have you been talking to?" Tim moved behind Sarah, his hands resting on her shoulders.

"No-one."

"You're lying." Tim's hands were round Sarah's neck now. "Tell me you're lying."

Sarah began to scream as his hands gripped her throat.

Chris and Jake were through the back door and into the kitchen before Sarah had a chance to scream again. She twisted round and slammed her chair hard against Tim's legs. He gave a grunt of pain and slackened his grip on her throat.

Meanwhile, Jake and Chris grabbed his arms and pinned him against the wall.

"Did you kill Anne because she was going to leave you?" asked Jake, his voice breaking. "Because you couldn't keep her, Tim?"

"Tell them." Sarah's voice was gentle. "You need help, Tim. A lot of help."

There was a long silence as Chris and Jake held Tim, his face pressed into the wall. But he made no attempt to struggle as his body went limp.

"I killed her," he said at long last. "Because I couldn't force her to stay and I couldn't bear to be alone."

****

Tim made a full confession at the police station. Then Sarah, Chris and Jake made their own painful statements.

****

Later that evening Chris and Sarah booked into a small hotel near the harbour.

"He could have murdered you too." Chris seemed more shocked than Sarah.

"I know that," said Sarah, gazing out of the window. She wondered if there was going to be a sunset that night. "I should never have trusted Tim so much. He must have been sick for a very long time."

Chris took her hand. "Would you come back to me? We could make a fresh start."

Sarah hesitated. Could that really happen? Suddenly she decided to be more forceful. She had been pushed around too much. She hoped that she wasn't going to allow that to happen again. "Maybe. You've got to give me time."

More Teen Titles!

Joe's Story by Rachel Anderson 1-902260-70-8

Playing Against the Odds by Bernard Ashley 1-902260-69-4

Harpies by David Belbin 1-842990-31-4

TWOCKING by Eric Brown 1-842990-42-X

To Be A Millionaire by Yvonne Coppard 1-902260-58-9

All We Know of Heaven by Peter Crowther 1-842990-32-2

Ring of Truth by Alan Durant 1-842990-33-0

Baby, Baby by Vivian French 1-842990-61-6

Falling Awake by Vivian French 1-902260-54-6

The Wedding Present by Adèle Geras 1-902260-77-5

The Cold Heart of Summer by Alan Gibbons 1-842990-81-0

Shadow on the Stairs by Ann Halam 1-902260-57-0

Alien Deeps by Douglas Hill 1-902260-55-4

Dade County's Big Summer by Lesley Howarth 1-842990-43-8

Runaway Teacher by Pete Johnson 1-902260-59-7

No Stone Unturned by Brian Keaney 1-842990-34-9

Wings by James Lovegrove 1-842990-11-X

A Kind of Magic by Catherine MacPhail 1-842990-10-1

Clone Zone by Jonathan Meres 1-842990-09-8

The Dogs by Mark Morris 1-902260-76-7

Turnaround by Alison Prince 1-842990-44-6

All Change by Rosie Rushton 1-902260-75-9

Fall Out by Rosie Rushton 1-842990-74-8

The Blessed and The Damned by Sara Sheridan 1-842990-08-X

Barrington Stoke, 10 Belford Terrace, Edinburgh EH4 3DQ
Tel: 0131 315 4933 Fax: 0131 315 4934
E-mail: info@barringtonstoke.co.uk
Website: www.barringtonstoke.co.uk

Become a Consultant!

Would you like to give us feedback on our titles before they are published? Contact us at the e-mail address below – we'd love to hear from you!

E-mail: info@barringtonstoke.co.uk
Website: www.barringtonstoke.co.uk